chronicle books • san francisco

Steam Train, Dream Train

SHERRI DUSKEY RINKER AND TOM LICHTENHELD

The **well cars** carry giant beasts
munching on enormous feasts.
Brachiosaurus likes the view,
while T-rex gets a bone to chew.

The **flatbed cars** are rolling beds.
The weary crew can rest their heads,
and settle in, and tuck in tight.
Their work is finished for tonight.

The red **caboose** is last in line—
from the lookout, all looks fine.

The freight and crew are tucked away.
The next stop . . . is another day.

A hiss, a jolt, a shift and sway,
now the journey's underway.
The train's departing, car by car.
The headlight fades into the stars.

Puffing, chuffing out of sight . . .

Steam train, dream train . . .
chhhhhh . . . goodnight.

To Dave, Ben, and Zak: Thank you for this amazing journey.
To my Dad, Ron Duskey, for a lifetime of love, support,
(mostly!) good advice, and the occasional harsh lecture.
And to my Father, who has led the way —S. D. R.

To my Dad, for being an artist and a gentleman. (And for
buying us *Mad* magazine.)
To my Mom, for encouraging my creativity and—to this
day—showing us what matters. —T. L.

Library of Congress Cataloging-in-Publication Data
Rinker, Sherri Duskey.
Steam train, dream train / by Sherri Duskey Rinker ; illustrated by
Tom Lichtenheld.
p. cm.
Summary: In this book with rhyming text, the dream train pulls into the
station and all the different cars are loaded by the animal workers, each
with the appropriate cargo.
ISBN 978-1-4521-0920-6 (alk. paper)
1. Railroad trains—Juvenile fiction. 2. Animals—Juvenile fiction. 3. Stories
in rhyme. [1. Stories in rhyme. 2. Railroad trains—Fiction. 3. Animals—Fiction.]
I. Lichtenheld, Tom, ill. II. Title.
PZ8.3.R48123Ste 2013
[E]—dc23
2012030942

Book design by Tom Lichtenheld and Kristine Brogno.
Typeset in Neutraface Slab.
The illustrations in this book were rendered in Neocolor wax oil pastels
on Mi-Teintes paper.

Manufactured in China.

10 9 8 7 6 5 4 3 2
Chronicle Books LLC
680 Second Street, San Francisco, California 94107

www.chroniclekids.com